"We're off to the market, Fergus!"
called Farmer Bob.
"Look after the animals and make sure
they don't get into any trouble."

He went through to the kitchen.
There were the pigs . . . eating spaghetti
and baked beans!

He rushed upstairs to the bedroom
to find the goat . . . wearing the new
hat and coat that Farmer Bob's wife
had just bought!

...the cow was taking a bubble bath!

"Phew! Just in time!" thought Fergus.
But had he forgotten anything? He tried
hard to remember. What about the cow . . .
. . . was she still in the bath?
Fergus groaned and closed his eyes.

Fr
JE Ma   c.1
MADDOX, TONY
 FERGUS'S UPSIDE-DOWN DAY

DATE DUE

JUL 3 0 1999		
AUG 0 7 1999		
AUG 1 6 1999		
AUG 3 1 1999		
SEP 0 3 1999		
JAN 0 5 2000		
JAN 2 0 2000		
MAY 2 7 2000		
JUL 1 7 2000		
DEC 1 4 2000		
JUN 3 0 2001		
JUL 2 1 2001		

GAYLORD M2